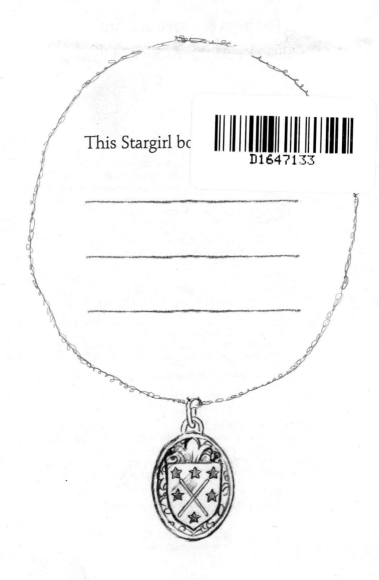

This Stargirl bo

_____

_____

_____

For my very special Stargirls,
Elise, Kezia, Dorothy and Amina

First published 2013 by Walker Books Ltd
87 Vauxhall Walk, London SE11 5HJ

2 4 6 8 10 9 7 5 3 1

Text © 2013 Vivian French
Illustrations © 2013 Jo Anne Davies

The right of Vivian French and Jo Anne Davies to be identified
as author and illustrator respectively of this work
has been asserted by them in accordance with the
Copyright, Designs and Patents Act 1988

This book has been typeset in StempelSchneidler

Printed and bound in Great Britain
by Clays Ltd, St Ives plc

British Library Cataloguing in Publication Data:
a catalogue record for this book is available from
the British Library

ISBN 978-1-4063-4527-8
www.walker.co.uk

Stargirl Academy

Emma's
Glittering Spell

VIVIAN FRENCH

WALKER
BOOKS

Stargirl Academy

Where magic makes a difference!

HEAD TEACHER
Fairy Mary McBee

DEPUTY HEAD
Miss Scritch

TEACHER
Fairy Fifibelle Lee

TEAM STARLIGHT

Lily

Madison

Sophie

Ava

Emma

Olivia

TEAM TWINSTAR

Melody

Jackson

Dear Stargirl,

Welcome to *Stargirl Academy*!

My name is Fairy Mary McBee, and I'm delighted you're here. All my Stargirls are very special, and I can tell that you are wonderful too.

We'll be learning how to use magic safely and efficiently to help anyone who is in trouble, but before we go any further I have a request. The Academy MUST be kept secret. This is VERY important...

So may I ask you to join our other Stargirls in making The Promise? Read it – say it out loud if you wish – then sign your name on the bottom line.

Thank you so much ... and well done!

Fairy Mary

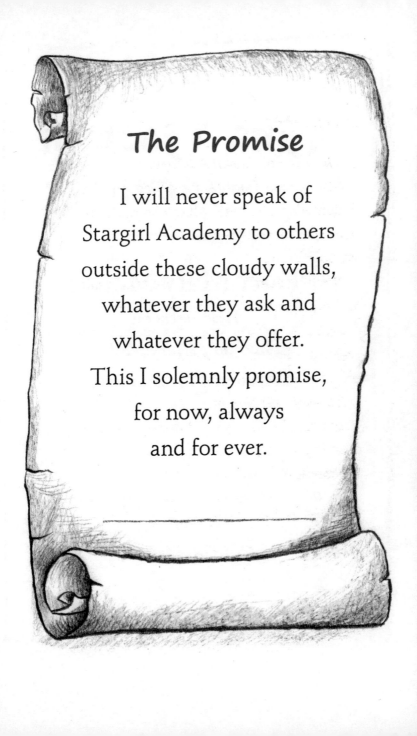

The Promise

I will never speak of
Stargirl Academy to others
outside these cloudy walls,
whatever they ask and
whatever they offer.
This I solemnly promise,
for now, always
and for ever.

The Book of Spells

by
Fairy Mary McBee

Head Teacher at

The Fairy Mary McBee
Academy for Stargirls

◆ ◆ ◆

A complete list of Spells can be obtained from the Academy.

Only the fully qualified need apply. Other applications

will be refused.

Glittering Spells

Glittering spells are for the more advanced student. Careful preparation is required, and it should be noted that each spell may only be used once unless a fully qualified Fairy Godmother is present and has given permission.

Important information:

- The only Glittering Spell available to students at the Fairy Mary McBee Academy for Stargirls is the Forgetting Spell
- Other Glittering Spells, such as Transformation, or Serious Addiction to Sleep, will not be taught in this Academy

Hello!

My name's Emma! Actually my full name is Emma Jane Susan Piefold.

I think my parents looked up the most boring names in the whole wide world and said, "Give us three of those. Any three – they'll do." My grandma told me that my mum and dad REALLY wanted a boy but they got me instead – and then they found out it was always going to be me on my own. Sometimes I wonder if they'd have given me a different name if they'd known I was going to be an only child. I'd love to be called Madison or Ava or Olivia or Sophie or Lily like my very special

Stargirl friends. Melody and Jackson are Stargirls too, but they aren't in our team. They think they're way better than we are. They aren't, though. Our team - Team Starlight - is the best EVER!

My mum doesn't think Emma is a boring name. She says it's pretty, and her most favourite book in the whole wide world is called Emma, and I should be very proud of having such a special name.

My mum knows a lot of things, and so does my dad. They're both teachers. But they don't know everything. They don't know how to stop Mr Appleby next door talking - not at all! I do. I just say, "Sorry, Mr Appleby - I've got to run!" And then I dash away at ninety miles an hour because once he starts he goes on and on and on for hours and hours and hours, and I can hear Mum saying, "Well..." and "I'm sure ..." and "I really MUST go..." But she never gets away unless I go and ring the front doorbell or Dad calls her from indoors. So you can see that I'd never describe Mr Appleby as my most favourite person ... but the weirdest things can happen when you're a Stargirl!

Love Emma XXX

Chapter One

Mr Appleby's our next-door neighbour and he has the most perfect garden – you'd think he polishes it every morning and every evening. The lawn has the neatest stripes, as if he's painted it rather than mown it, but he still has loads of time to lean over the fence and chat. His latest thing is complaining about the new family that's just moved in to the house next to his. Apparently the little boys play football indoors, and the baby keeps on crying.

Mum says Mr A talks a lot because he's lonely, but I think it's the other way round and he's lonely because everyone knows how much he talks, and so (like me) they

15

run away when they see him coming.

Anyway, last Saturday Mum was being talked at in the garden and I was picking up windfall apples under the tree when I got the most ENORMOUS Tingle in my elbow. Do you know what that means? It means it's time to go to Stargirl Academy, which is the most exciting thing EVER to happen to me. We go to the Academy and learn SPELLS!

By the way, you have to absolutely promise never to tell anyone about the Academy because the head teacher Fairy Mary McBee told us it was the most enormous secret. Is that OK? I'm sure it is.

So I had this huge Tingle – my elbow positively HURT – and I thought, Hurrah!

I told Mum I was taking the apples inside and I ran into the house through the back door, only instead of ending up in the

messy back room where we keep the washing machine, guess what? I found myself in the corridor of Stargirl Academy!

Lily and Madison and some of the others say it gets misty before they find the Academy front door, but I've never had that happen to me. Well, only a few little wisps of fog. In a way it's strange that I DON'T see any mist, because the Academy rests on the top of an enormous cloud and floats around ... in fact, a long time ago it was called Cloudy Towers. That was when it was an academy for training Fairy God-mothers, but now it's been brought up to date and Fairy Mary McBee is training us to be Stargirls instead. I'm so very glad she de-cided on the change. Sometimes I look at the secret glowing star on the tip of my littlest left hand finger, and I feel as if I'm glowing myself – glowing with happiness! We were given our secret stars on our very first visit, and we use our star fingers when we're casting a spell – isn't that amazing?

It's a VERY exciting life being a Stargirl. One minute I was in our garden, and the next minute – woweee! – I was on my way to meet up with the three Fairy Godmothers who teach us magic. I still had the bag of apples in my hand as I went into the workroom where we meet and have our lessons.

Fairy Fifibelle Lee and Miss Scritch were both there when I walked in. Miss Scritch is the deputy head, and Fairy Fifibelle is a teacher. I like Fairy Fifibelle loads because she doesn't always get things right, and that makes me feel much better because I don't either, although I always try my best. I'm a little bit afraid of Miss Scritch. She can be scary and she doesn't like it when I talk too much, which I do sometimes. Our head teacher, Fairy Mary McBee, is LOVELY! But she wasn't there, and neither were any of my friends.

"Oh!" I said. "Am I the first?"

Miss Scritch nodded. "Unless someone is hiding under the table, Emma, you are undoubtedly the first Stargirl to arrive today."

I wasn't sure if I was meant to laugh or not, so I made a sort of agreeing noise. Sometimes it's difficult to tell if Miss Scritch is joking or being sarcastic.

Fairy Fifibelle Lee beamed at me. "It's wonderful to see you, dearest Emma. Are you ready for a special day today?"

I smiled back. "I hope so! Why is it special?"

"Fairy Mary McBee will tell you when she comes in," Fairy Fifibelle promised. "Why don't we go and wait in the sitting-room? I'm sure the others won't be long."

I was pleased, because I adore the sitting-room. The workroom is very interesting with all its bulging cupboards full of

21

magical bits and pieces, and its shelves of bottles and jars, but it isn't a place to sit in and relax. The sitting-room is completely different. The walls are covered in the funniest pictures, mostly of the Fairy Godmothers who were trained here years ago. Sometimes they wave at us, and there's one who often gives me a little wink in a friendly kind of way. There's always a roaring fire, and the sofas and chairs are incredibly comfortable. It's the kind of room that makes you feel comfy inside yourself as well as outside, if you know what I mean.

I snuggled down on the biggest sofa, and Fairy Fifibelle sat down opposite me. "Tell me, dearest, how are you getting on?" she said. "Are you enjoying yourself?"

"I LOVE it here!" I told her. "I love everything about being a Stargirl – I love having a star finger and my friends and I love learning magic and spells—Oh, and I totally love my necklace!"

Our necklaces are very special indeed.
Fairy Mary McBee gave us one each
when we first came to the Academy, and
they're truly magical. If we tap them, we
turn invisible! Well, we can just about see
each other, and our Fairy Godmothers
can always see us, but we're invisible to
ordinary people. And the necklaces aren't
just magical. They're very pretty too.
I never get tired of looking at the Academy
crest on the pendant with its two crossed
wands and six little twinkling stars.

Even though the sitting-room wasn't
brightly lit, four out of the six stars
twinkled back at me as I gave my pendant a
little polish, and I sighed happily.

"I can't believe I'll be a fully qualified
Stargirl soon," I said. "Only two more
stars." A sudden doubt came into my mind,

and I gave Fairy Fifibelle an anxious smile. "That is right, isn't it?"

Fairy Fifibelle Lee nodded. "Of course, my precious petal. 'For every good deed done, a star will shine.' That's the Stargirl Academy rule."

"Everyone in Team Starlight has four stars now," I told her, and then I hesitated. Had Melody and Jackson got four stars? I wasn't sure. They weren't part of our team; when they first came to the Academy, they'd announced they were going to be a team of two, and they always behave as if they're MUCH better than we are ... but I don't think they are. Not really, even though they're very good at magic.

Fairy Fifibelle gave me another of her beaming smiles. "Fairy Mary and Miss Scritch and I are delighted with the way

you work together to help people, and we're sure you'll graduate very soon. When all six of your stars are shining, there'll be a party to celebrate, and Fairy Mary McBee will give you your certificates!"

I love parties, and I was sure a party at Stargirl Academy would be brilliant fun, but before I could say anything there was the sound of laughter and Fairy Fifibelle looked up. "That sounds like the other Stargirls," she said. "Shall we go and join them?"

Chapter Two

Fairy Fifibelle was right. The others had arrived, and so had Fairy Mary McBee — and there was a stranger in the workroom. A very small round man with snow-white hair, bristly eyebrows and bright blue eyes was sitting at the end of the table. He was chatting to Miss Scritch, and for once she was smiling — and I was surprised to see she looked quite pretty. As Fairy Fifibelle and I walked in, she actually laughed at something the little man said!

"Emma!" Fairy Mary gave a welcoming wave. "This is Professor Moth. He's come to show you how to cast a Forgetting Spell."

Melody was leaning against the wall, and

she raised her eyebrows the way she does when she wants to look grown-up and cool. "A Forgetting Spell?" she drawled. "Won't we forget it as soon as we've learnt it?"

The professor chuckled, and wiggled his fingers at her. "All will be revealed, little Miss Melody! Be patient, and together we will learn a splendid new skill!"

I wanted to laugh because Melody's face was such a mixture of astonishment and fury. I don't suppose anybody had called her "little miss" for years. I didn't laugh, though, because I knew that would make her even more furious, and she's scary when she's angry.

The professor wasn't scared in the least. "Good morning, all young ladies. Excuse me one little moment, whilst we get to know each other." He sat back in his chair and

looked carefully at each of us in turn, and when it was my turn I was quite certain he could see right inside my head. It was the strangest feeling! It must have showed on my face – or maybe he read it in my thoughts – because he said, "Aha! Miss Emma! There is no need to worry. Your head is oh so very full of wonderful words. You like to talk, I think. I am right, yes?"

All my friends laughed, and so did Fairy Mary and Fairy Fifibelle, and even Miss Scritch smiled. I tried not to blush, but it was difficult. "I do try not to talk too much," I said, "but it just kind of comes out before I can stop myself and once I've started I find it really difficult to stop – but I'm not as bad as Mr Appleby next door. He really DOES go on and on and—" I stopped, because I realised I was sounding EXACTLY like

Mr Appleby. "Ooops!" I said. "Sorry..."

"Talking is not bad always," the professor said, "and your heart is most truthful." He raised one of his hands. "Fairy Mary McBee, do I have your most gracious permission? I wish to ask these girls to show me the spells already learned."

Fairy Mary nodded. "Of course, Professor. Would you like a cup of tea before you begin?"

Professor Moth's blue eyes brightened. "What I would like more than anything, dear Fairy Mary, is a mug of your excellent hot chocolate. The Stargirl Academy is famous for the hot chocolate. And a biscuit, perhaps, if such a thing you have?"

"I'm sure we can do better than a biscuit," Fairy Mary told him. "Miss Scritch, could you see what we have in the kitchen cupboard? And we'll all have hot chocolate.

It'll make a nice start to the day."

Miss Scritch, who had been gazing at the professor as if he was the most amazing person she'd ever seen, jumped. "Yes, Fairy Mary. I'll see to it at once. I'll just run and fetch my wand."

She hurried out of the workroom, and Madison dug her elbow into my side. "I think Miss Scritch likes him!" she whispered.

"I do too," I whispered back, and then realised the professor was looking straight at us.

"Miss Madison and Miss Emma," he said, "perhaps you would now put your very interesting observations to one side. I wish to see a fine example of the Floating Spell."

Madison and I both went scarlet, and looked hastily around for something to

float. Jackson had put her pencil case on the table, and I pointed my star finger at it.

As I did so, I thought of all the floatiest things I could – feathers and clouds and birds and butterflies. At once, the case floated upwards, but a moment later it turned upside down and all the pencils fell out.

Luckily, Madison, her eyes screwed up behind her glasses in concentration, was already pointing at the pencils. They stopped half a centimetre away from the table top, hesitated, then floated back up to hover beside the case.

"Wonderful!" Professor Moth clapped loudly. "This is well done, well done indeed."

"That's EASY," Jackson said. "Watch this!" She pointed her star finger, and the pencils popped back inside the case – and the zip closed in a series of tiny jerks. Jackson reached out, caught the pencil case and put it back on the table in front of her.

"WOW!" Sophie was wide-eyed. "How did you make the zip do that?"

Jackson shrugged. "Natural genius. Some of us have it, and some of us don't."

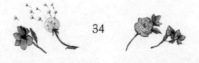

I thought the professor would be impressed, but he didn't seem to have noticed. He turned to Sophie and Lily, and asked them to demonstrate the Solidifying Spell. Sophie pulled a ribbon out of her pocket, and she and Lily pointed their star fingers at it. We each tried to pick it up in turn, but they'd done really well. The ribbon was so heavy that none of us could get it to move at all, until Melody tried. She managed to lift it a few centimetres before she dropped it again with a loud BANG!

Jackson grinned at her. "Clever Melody!"

"See?" Melody was pleased with herself. "They didn't do it that well!"

The professor raised one of his bristly eyebrows. "It is not so clever, I think, if someone makes weaker the original spell.

35

It is not so clever if someone—" he looked straight at Melody— "casts a tiny, tiny Floating Spell to make the Solidifying Spell not so strong."

"I didn't do any such thing," Melody protested.

I didn't entirely believe her. And I'm not sure the professor did either, but he was interrupted by Miss Scritch.

"Snack time!" she announced. She sat down beside Professor Moth and waved her wand. At once trays of cake and sandwiches and biscuits covered the table, together with bowls of trifle and jelly and at least seven different flavours of ice cream. Mugs of steaming hot chocolate came twirling out of the air and settled between the trays, and a heap of marshmallows poured into an empty bowl until it was overflowing.

"Wonderful! Such wonderful magic!" The professor beamed at Miss Scritch, and she looked modestly down at her wand.

"It's nothing," she said. "Do please help yourself."

Chapter Three

I found myself wishing Professor Moth came to the Academy every day. Miss Scritch had really gone to town – we'd never had such an amazing amount of food before, and everything tasted completely delicious. Normally our deputy head doesn't approve of too many treats, but it was obvious that she was trying to impress our visitor. She was fluttering round him and smiling from ear to ear. I thought it was really sweet to see her like that – she's usually so stern and sour-looking – but I saw Melody rolling her eyes at Jackson, and Jackson made a horrible face back. Luckily Miss Scritch was too busy giving the professor double

helpings of everything on the table to notice.

I've never seen anyone eat as much as Professor Moth did. He ate nearly all the trifle by himself, and most of the sandwiches, as well as half of each of the cakes, and he drank at least six mugs of hot chocolate. Miss Scritch was glowing with pride as he finally put down his fork and said, "I cannot eat one more thing. I am as stuffed full as the Christmas dumpling!"

I don't think any of us knew what he meant, but we smiled politely as we started to pile up the plates and mugs.

"Permit me to help you in your tidiness," the professor said, and he pulled a small shiny wand from his pocket. Before Fairy Mary or Miss Scritch could say a word, he'd waved it at the table and – WHOOOMPH! – everything was gone.

39

"Erm..." Fairy Mary smiled a not entirely enthusiastic smile. "That's very kind of you."

Professor Moth clutched at his head. "I have done wrong! I can see! You do the washing-up here, is that not so? I forget these modern customs."

"Well ... yes, actually," Fairy Mary said.

"I will reverse! See? It can be done – SO!" Professor Moth waved his wand a second time, and every plate and mug reappeared – but spotlessly clean. Gleaming, in fact.

Miss Scritch jumped up and clapped wildly. "Miraculous!"

The professor gave her a small bow, and she looked delighted. Fairy Mary nodded at Fairy Fifibelle, who waved her wand and the crockery and cutlery flew swiftly away.

"Shall we continue, Professor?" Fairy Mary suggested. "You were about to ask Ava and

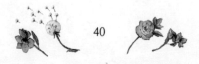

Olivia to show you the Sliding Spell, were you not?"

Professor Moth looked surprised, then nodded. "Yes. Young ladies, please oblige."

Ava picked up a pen and drew a smiley face on the back of her hand before she and Olivia pointed their Star Fingers. The smiley face slid first to Sophie's hand, then mine, then Lily's. Jackson and Melody were

whispering together and not paying much attention so Olivia left them out, but the smiley face slid on round the table until Ava had it back again.

The professor twinkled at Fairy Mary, Miss Scritch and Fairy Fifibelle Lee. "You teach your pupils exceedingly well," he said. "And there is one more spell, I think?"

"It's the Copying Spell," Melody told him, and before she was even asked she and Jackson pointed their fingers first at Miss Scritch, then at me ... and something DREADFUL happened. So dreadful it makes me feel weird even now to think about it. All of a sudden, I was on my feet, clapping wildly and calling out, "Miraculous!" exactly the way Miss Scritch had done, even though every bit of me was trying desperately not to. I saw Miss Scritch go pale, but Fairy Mary put out her hand.

"That," she said calmly, "is enough!" Her wand flickered between her fingers, there was a shower of shining stars, and I sank into my seat.

Professor Moth rose to his feet. "This is not good use of a spell!"

"Indeed it isn't," Fairy Mary said. "Jackson and Melody, you will please leave the room. Go next door. Now."

Chapter Four

There was a shocked silence. We hardly dared to breathe as Melody and Jackson got up from the table and walked towards the sitting-room. They both looked very shaken, and at the door Melody turned. "It was only a joke," she said. "We didn't mean any harm."

"Making fun of people hurts their feelings," Fairy Mary told her, "and Stargirls don't do that. Not ever." Her voice was cold. "I'd like you both to think long and hard about whether you deserve to remain at the Academy."

Melody went silently out of the room, and Jackson followed her. Fairy Mary McBee

closed her eyes for a moment, then opened them. "I think it must be time for Professor Moth to show us the Forgetting Spell," she said.

The professor was tugging at his thick white hair. "Such a waste of good talent," he said. "Those girls! They have skills at magic, and I do not think their hearts are all bad."

"I don't think so either," Fairy Mary said. "But they need to understand there is more to being a Stargirl than being good at spells. Shall we continue?"

Professor Moth gave his hair one last tug. "I understand. It is not for me to discuss this little incident. You are right. We should continue. Young ladies? Let us lift up our star fingers."

We held up our little fingers, and the tiny

stars glowed as Professor Moth held up his own hand. There was a star on his little finger too, and it was shining so brightly I could see it from right across the room.

"Jeepers creepers," Lily whispered. "Is he a Fairy Godfather?"

Fairy Mary McBee put her finger to her lips, but she nodded as she did so. "A very special Fairy Godfather," she said softly.

The professor hadn't noticed Lily's interruption. "Listen with all your ears," he said. "This spell is to be used on one person to wipe from the mind all that has just happened. What is it you would say? Ah, yes! It will delete the memory that is most recent. And also, this spell can be used the one time only; one time, and then it is gone." He waved a hand in the air. "And now we are ready. Say after me, *Memory*

47

hold not, memory care not, memory slip slide slither away..."

We repeated his words slowly and carefully, and the professor nodded as a flurry of glittering sparkles swirled round his head. "This is good. Keep up your hands." He walked round the table, and as he came to each of us he touched our tiny glowing stars.

When it was my turn I jumped; my little finger felt red-hot, and a Tingle buzzed in my elbow.

"Good." Professor Moth went back to his seat. "So now the spell is safe within your heads. Again the words, if you please?"

"*Memory hold not, memory care not, memory slip slide slither away...*" we chorused.

"That is correct." The professor folded his arms. "Now, please to use this only when it is truly necessary to delete the memory. As I have told you, it will work once in a day, so we will have no practising. There are many types of spell; this is of the type Glittering. Puff! and it is gone."

Miss Scritch gave Professor Moth a congratulatory pat on the back. "A fine example of how to teach," she said, and she gave Fairy Fifibelle Lee a sideways glance. "Some of us are not so precise."

Fairy Fifibelle looked offended. "We all have our different styles," she said.

"Indeed we do," Fairy Mary agreed. "Just like our Stargirls. It would be extremely dull if we were all the same. Professor Moth, I wonder if you would do us the honour of joining us for the Spin?"

"You will do the Spin?" The professor looked as if he'd been given a wonderful present. "I did not think there were any people left who do this!"

Miss Scritch hurried to where Fairy Mary McBee's Golden Wand was hanging on the wall, and placed it on the table in front of the professor. He touched it gently, as if it was very precious, then handed it to our head teacher. "This is your magic, most honourable Fairy Mary. The magic of the Fairy Godmothers."

I watched as Fairy Mary put the wand down. The Spin is the most extraordinary part of our day at the Academy; it's when we find out who will choose what sort of adventure we're going to go on, and who we're going to help. It's very strange and magical ... but something didn't feel right.

51

We weren't all there, and it made me uncomfortable. After all, weren't Stargirls meant to look after each other, and work together?

"Please, Fairy Mary," I said. "What about Jackson and Melody? Aren't they going to be here for the Spin?"

"Darling girl!" Fairy Fifibelle swooped down and gave me one of her famous hugs where you get buried in fluttering scarves and floaty sleeves and ribbons. "Such thought for others!"

Miss Scritch didn't sound nearly so enthusiastic. "Really, Emma! Surely you don't think Melody and Jackson deserve to be here?"

I wriggled in my chair. "I don't know. That is, I know they SO shouldn't have made fun of you, but sometimes they do things because they want to look clever and they haven't thought about what'll happen afterwards or how it'll make people feel. But the Spin is so very special that they'll feel terrible at being left out..." I stopped. I was talking too much, again.

Everyone was staring at me, except Fairy Mary McBee. She was looking thoughtful. "Does anyone else think Melody and Jackson should take part in the Spin?" she asked.

Olivia put up her hand, but I could see Madison and Ava and Lily hesitating. Sophie shook her head. "I'd say they should be left alone while they think about what they've done."

Fairy Mary turned back to me. "Well, Emma? Is Sophie right, do you think?"

Chapter Five

"Erm…" I bit my lip while I tried to make up my mind. I thought about how I'd feel if I knew that the Spin was happening without me, and I knew that I'd be completely miserable … but maybe Sophie was being sensible, and Jackson and Melody *did* need some time without interruptions. It was all so difficult that I sighed the most enormous sigh.

That made the professor laugh, but it was a kind laugh. "She does much thinking, this little Emma," he said.

I was already thinking about something else, but I didn't like to mention it. Melody and Jackson hadn't learnt the spell; did that

mean they wouldn't be able to win another star on their pendants? My stomach went into knots at such an awful idea.

Madison leant against my arm. "Do you think they'll get to go out with us when we've chosen who to help?" she whispered.

"I don't know," I whispered back.

"No whispering!" Miss Scritch gave us a stern look. "Fairy Mary, shall we continue?"

Fairy Mary was still looking thoughtful. "Emma, dear, why don't you pop your head round the door and see how Melody and Jackson are getting on?"

Miss Scritch looked horrified. "Is that REALLY a good idea, Headmistress?"

"I think it might be," Fairy Mary said.

Fairy Fifibelle nodded. "Darling Emma." I rather suspected she was going to give me another hug, so I got up quickly and headed

for the sitting-room. I opened the door very quietly, and peeped in.

Melody and Jackson were sitting close together on the sofa ... but they weren't alone. Three of the Fairy Godmothers had climbed out of their picture frames and were sitting with them, and judging by the look on Melody's face, they'd been giving her and Jackson a terrible telling-off.

Jackson was blowing her nose, and Melody was very pink around the eyes.

"They won't want me to see them looking like that," I thought.

I was about to tiptoe out again when one of the Fairy Godmothers looked up and saw me. "Goodness!" she said. "We have an observer! Come along, girls. I think we've said enough. Off we go!" And she and the

other two ancient ladies hopped up off their seats amidst a shower of twinkly little stars and when I looked again they were back on the wall.

"Thanks, Emma." Jackson put her hankie back in her pocket. "I thought they were never going to stop talking."

"I'm sorry to interrupt," I said. "I didn't know there'd be anyone else here with you."

Melody shook her head. "They were waiting for us."

"They made us feel as if we've been really mean," Jackson said with a sniff. "Did you know Miss Scritch looked after her ancient mother for years and years and years, and couldn't take the final Fairy Godmother exam? THAT'S why she's Miss Scritch and not Fairy Angelica."

"Oh," I said. I'd never even thought to wonder about Miss Scritch's name.

Melody pushed back her hair. "So we're going to tell her that we're sorry. And we are, aren't we, Jackson?"

"Yes," Jackson said. "We are."

"Perhaps you'd better come back," I suggested. "We're about to do the Spin."

"Really? We haven't missed it?" Melody brightened. "What about learning the Forgetting Spell?"

I shook my head. "Sorry. Actually, we've just done that."

Melody shrugged. "Well, at least we haven't missed everything. Come on, Jackson."

She took Jackson's hand, and they walked past me into the workroom. As I followed after them I heard a cracked old voice

behind me ask, "Do you believe them, Fairy Roseberry? Are they genuinely sorry?"

And an even older voice answered, "They think they are, Tottie dear. But we'll see what we see."

Back in the workroom, Jackson went straight to Miss Scritch. "I want to apologise," she said.

"We both do," Melody added. "And we don't want to leave the Academy— " her voice suddenly wobbled— "because we do want to be Stargirls." She glanced at Fairy Mary McBee. "If you'll let us have another chance, that is."

Fairy Mary picked up the Golden Wand from the table. "What do you think, Miss Scritch?"

Miss Scritch hesitated, and looked at the professor. He was staring upwards as if

there was something very interesting about the bunches of herbs that were hanging from the ceiling. Miss Scritch coughed, but he still took no notice.

"Hm," she said at last. "I think you both have ability. Real ability. So I accept your apology."

"Such generosity!" Fairy Fifibelle Lee floated across the room, but Miss Scritch sidestepped her neatly and avoided the oncoming hug.

The professor smiled. "A right decision indeed, I think."

Miss Scritch's cheeks went pink. "I do hope so."

"Then that's settled." Fairy Mary sounded relieved. "Take your places, Melody and Jackson, and we'll begin."

Chapter Six

I absolutely LOVE the Spin. It's so very magical, and it sends little shivers up and down my spine. The room goes dark and mysterious when Fairy Mary McBee begins, and none of us knows how it happens ... but you can feel the magic in the air.

This time it grew even darker than usual, and the Golden Wand glowed incredibly brightly as it spun round and round and round. It made a low humming sound that got right inside my head and made me feel as if I was humming too.

"Spin, spin, spin," Fairy Mary sang softly. "Who will choose? Who will it be? Whose

destiny will change today? Spin, wand, spin..."

We watched and watched, and still the wand went on spinning. Just as I thought it was going to go on for ever, the humming grew fainter, and then, with a sudden jerk, the wand stopped dead.

Who was it pointing at?

Me!

The daylight came back into the room as if someone had clicked a switch.

We rubbed our eyes, and Lily patted me on the back. "It's your turn, Emma! Who do you want to help?"

I didn't know what to say. It may sound silly, but I'd never expected to be chosen. When the wand pointed at Madison and Ava and Jackson, they knew at once who

they wanted to help, but I didn't have a clue. "Erm…" I said. "I'm not sure…"

Melody frowned at me. "Come on, Emma. You must be able to think of someone." Jackson elbowed her, and Melody changed her frown into a smile. "I mean, you must know somebody who's in trouble?"

The only person I could think of was Mr Appleby, and I wasn't sure he exactly needed help; it was more the people around him who needed help to get away from him! "Erm…" I said again. "There's a man who lives next door who talks a lot."

Jackson gave me one of her despising stares and began to say something, but then she saw Fairy Mary looking at her, and she hastily changed it to a question. "What does he talk about?"

"He's always complaining about the family next door," I told her. "I don't know them – they've only just moved in – but he says they're ever so noisy. He says the two boys play football up and down the stairs and never go out, and the baby cries all night and keeps him awake."

Olivia gave me a beaming smile. "It sounds to me as if they're the ones who need us!"

Sophie nodded. "Poor little baby."

Fairy Fifibelle Lee leant across the table. "May I make a suggestion, darling Emma?" she said. "Why don't you take the Travelling Tower and find out a little more about your neighbours? Moving into a new house is always difficult, and the family may well need your help."

I thought that sounded like a brilliant idea, and I said so.

Madison took off her spectacles, and waved them in the air. "Stargirls to the rescue!"

"That's settled, then," Fairy Mary said. "Professor, would you like a cup of coffee in the sitting-room? There's a spell Miss Scritch and I are considering teaching our girls sometime in the future, and we'd very much value your opinion."

The professor gave a little bow. "I would indeed be most honoured!"

Miss Scritch took his arm. "No, no," she said. "*We* are honoured to have *you* here!" And she marched him away.

If Fairy Fifibelle Lee felt left out, she didn't show it. She gathered us round her. "My chickens," she said. "Have you all got your necklaces on? In case you need to be invisible?" Of course we had. I don't think any of us ever take them off; they're much too precious. Fairy Fifibelle clicked her fingers, and a wonderfully shimmery scarf came drifting down from the ceiling. She wrapped it round her head and shoulders, then floated her way to the door. "Sweet girls. Follow me to the Travelling Tower!"

We followed her through the sitting-room, and saw Miss Scritch sitting next to the professor, waving her hands about as she talked. He was smiling politely, but Fairy Mary was dozing. I had a quick look up at the portraits of the old Fairy Godmothers, and most of them were asleep as well.

"It can't be a very interesting spell," Madison whispered, and I had to try hard not to laugh.

Chapter Seven

"Why is Fairy Fifibelle showing us the way?" Jackson wanted to know as we left the sitting-room and walked into the corridor on the other side. "We've done this loads of times."

"We did get lost once," Lily reminded her.

Jackson frowned. "Only by mistake. We're not babies. Doesn't she understand that?"

Melody pulled at her arm. "Sh, Jackson."

"What?" Jackson looked at her friend in surprise.

"We've got to be good," Melody warned her. "Don't be so argumentative!"

Jackson flushed. "Oops! Sorry."

"It's OK," Melody said. "I don't think Fairy Fifibelle heard you. She's singing too loudly."

It was true. Fairy Fifibelle Lee was floating through the long dark corridor singing a strange wordless song as she went. It sounded like a spell; it made me feel happy, but in a calm and contented kind of way.

"Have you noticed the lights?" Ava said in my ear. "Watch as she goes past ... they change colour!"

Ava was quite right. The lights glowed a soft raspberry pink as Fairy Fifibelle came near, but once she had floated by they went back to being yellow.

"I think she's really clever at magic," Ava went on. "She may get things wrong, but she knows some fabulous spells."

I was about to agree, but Fairy Fifibelle opened the door to the Travelling Tower and the sudden burst of sunlight made me blink and forget what I was going to say.

"There, my darlings! Off you go, and have a wonderful time." Fairy Fifibelle waved us inside. "And remember, the Forgetting Spell only works once." She waved again – and disappeared. She didn't fade or gradually turn invisible. One minute she was standing by the door, her drifty scarves floating around her, and the next minute she was gone.

I wasn't terribly surprised; once you're at Stargirl Academy, you get used to the weirdest things happening, but I did wonder why she hadn't just floated away down the corridor.

"WOW!" Madison rushed forward to

75

look out through the glass walls. "We're flying over a river!"

I went to stand beside her, and the view was wonderful. The Travelling Tower has glass walls all the way round, so if there wasn't a comfortingly solid floor under your feet, it would feel as if you were flying. It's attached to Stargirl Academy most of the time, but it's like a very amazing and magic kind of lift. It can go up and down, but it can also leave the Academy completely. Olivia hates it when that happens; she says she worries that we'll never get back again, but I know we will. Fairy Mary McBee would never put us in danger. As I looked out, I could clearly see the river below us, and a battered old iron bridge, and a cluster of houses and shops on the other side ... and then we went a little

further, and I thought, "I know where we are! That's my road down there."

The TT slowed right down, and I was able to point out my house to the others and to show them Mr Appleby's neat and tidy garden. It was interesting seeing it from above; I'd never realised how much bigger than our garden it was. And the garden next

door – where the new people lived – was bigger still, but it was SO different! The grass was long, and the flower beds were totally overgrown, and there was rubbish and bits of broken furniture everywhere. The only clear space was a tiny square behind the back door where an old woman was sitting on a chair in the sunshine. She was holding a baby, and singing as it wriggled in her arms.

"That's a pretty baby," Lily said. "Do you know what her name is?"

I shook my head. "I've never been to the house."

"Didn't you go and say hello when they moved in?" Olivia sounded so surprised I felt terrible. Mum and Dad had mentioned there were new people on our side of the road, but when I heard they didn't have any children my age I'd forgotten about them. I looked down at the baby, and Lily was right. She was really cute! And her grandmother looked nice too, although she looked anxious as well. The baby was crying, and it didn't seem as if she could soothe it.

A woman of about my mum's age came out and picked the baby up from the old woman's lap. "Poor little Baby Faye," she said. "Are your teeth still hurting?"

"Where are the boys, Poppy?" the old woman asked. "Shouldn't they be outside on a lovely day like this?"

Poppy sighed. "How can they play in this mess?" she asked. "There's so much rubbish all over the place, and some of it's broken glass – they'd be sure to cut themselves. And the grass is so long, and we've nothing to cut it with. Oh, Mum … why

did we move here? It's a lovely house, but the garden's much too big ... it makes me depressed just looking at it."

The old woman stretched out her hand to her daughter, and I suddenly realised she couldn't see. "Is it so very bad?"

"Terrible." Poppy buried her nose in the back of the baby's neck. "And the man next door hates us, and I don't blame him – Faye's cried every night since we got here."

"She'll be fine once her teeth come through," the old woman said, and she pulled herself to her feet. "You sit here a moment, and enjoy the sunshine. I'll make us a cup of tea."

"It's OK. I'll come in with you," Poppy said, and she took the old woman's arm and helped her inside.

"They really do need help," Sophie said. "Come on, Emma! What shall we do?"

I was thinking as hard as I could. It was obvious that we had to do something about the garden ... but what? And how? I knew nothing about gardening ... but then again, I did know someone who knew a LOT!

Chapter Eight

It was all very well knowing that Mr Appleby would be the perfect person to help us tidy up the garden, but how could we get him to see that? He didn't even like his neighbours.

"We can still help," Lily suggested, when I explained what the problem was. "We could tidy up the rubbish. You don't need to know anything about gardens to do that."

"Pick up rubbish?" Jackson looked horrified. "We'll get filthy!"

"We can use Floating Spells," Olivia pointed out.

Jackson shrugged. "I suppose so."

Madison, who always thinks of the

83

practical side of things, wanted to know where we were going to put the rubbish. "We can't dump it anywhere the boys might find it," she said. "Especially if there's broken glass."

"There's space behind that old shed in the corner," Sophie said. "It looks as if people have been burning stuff there already."

"Sorted." Madison looked approving.

The TT had dropped down to the level of the bedroom windows, and now we were closer I could see that the garden must once have been very pretty. There were loads of flowers fighting the weeds, and a beautiful rose was doing its best to survive in the middle of a heap of bits of smashed-up cupboard.

"Right," I said, and I folded my arms to make myself look as if I was in charge, although I didn't feel as if I was. "Shall we try some Floating Spells?"

We took it in turns to point our star fingers, and it was amazing how quickly we got rid of the broken furniture. Eight Stargirls can do a lot when they're all working together – although there were a couple of

times when I did have a tiny suspicion that Fairy Fifibelle Lee might not have disappeared as completely as we thought. I don't think any of us could have collected up the bits of broken glass, tipped them into a cardboard box, then floated the box away over the wall and into a skip that was standing outside a house on the other side of the road. I asked Olivia what she thought, and she smiled.

"Fairy Fifibelle's very kind," she said. "I wouldn't be surprised."

Melody heard us talking. "How do you know it wasn't me or Jackson?" she demanded. "We're much the best at the Floating Spell!"

I knew that was true, so I didn't say anything else about Fairy Fifibelle ... but I was almost sure I could hear murmuring, and it wasn't any of us Stargirls.

I whispered, "Thank you!"

There was no answer, but for a moment I felt something very soft and floaty brush against my cheek.

There was a huge heap of rubbish in the corner of the garden by the time we'd finished, but Madison said it would be OK. "They can have a fabulous bonfire," she said. "It's not too near anything that's going to catch light."

"That sounds fun," I said. "I love bonfires!"

"Maybe they'll ask you round," Sophie suggested, and I thought that I'd like that.

"It's looking ever so much better," I said. "If only we could get the grass cut, that would be brilliant." And then, as if he'd heard me, Mr Appleby stumped out into the garden next door, and pulled his motor mower out of his shed.

87

"WOW!" Ava's eyes lit up. "That's some mower! Would it work on long grass?"

I didn't know. It was one of those mowers you sit on, and it looked like it could take on a jungle; Mr Appleby absolutely loved it. I think he was disappointed that his grass didn't grow six inches every night.

Madison was watching him climb onto the seat. "I don't suppose…" she said, then stopped.

"…that we could float Mr Appleby and his mower over the fence?" Ava finished her sentence for her.

"He'd think he'd gone mad!" Olivia stared at Ava.

Lily had an idea. "But we could use the Forgetting Spell! Once he'd mowed the lawn, we could float him back, and then make him forget all about it!"

"But won't he get off the mower as soon as he finds himself in the wrong garden?" Sophie asked.

Jackson began to laugh. "Not if we put a Solidifying Spell on his clothes so he can't get off!"

"Isn't that a bit unkind?" Olivia looked at me, and I hesitated. I couldn't think of any other way of getting the grass cut, unless we did it ourselves, and we didn't have a mower. We didn't even have a pair of scissors! But on the other hand, it didn't feel right to make Mr Appleby do something like that.

"I don't know," I said slowly. "Perhaps we

can think of some way of persuading him, so he thinks it's his idea..."

Melody snorted. "You lot! Honestly! I don't see what you're making such a fuss about. If you won't do it, Jackson and I will. Here goes!"

And before I could say a word, she and Jackson were pointing their star fingers, and Mr Appleby and his mower were floating in a shower of shimmering stars...

...up...

...up...

...and over the fence.

Chapter Nine

I wasn't just horrified, I was completely and utterly terrified. What if the mower crashed? What if Mr Appleby fell off? For one wild moment, I thought of putting a Solidifying Spell on him, but I didn't. It would have made things even worse for sure.

All I could do was cross my fingers and hold my breath as the mower and its rider landed smoothly in the middle of the knee-high grass. The engine was still running, and the mower took off in the direction of the house, leaving a wonderfully close-mown path behind it.

I could hardly bear to look. I was certain

Mr Appleby would either be purple with rage or green with terror ... but when I finally forced myself to look, I had to blink hard, then look again.

His eyes were shut! It's true! There were still a few stars circling around him, so maybe it was something to do with the Floating Spell. His face was blank, as if he was asleep, but he couldn't have been because the mower turned at the edge of the lawn and went back the other way. To and fro it went, until there was only one little area of rough grass left...

And *that* was when the old lady came out of the back door of the house. She stood listening, and then the most wonderful smile spread over her face as she clapped her hands. "Thank you!" she called out. "Thank you a million times, whoever you are!"

Mr Appleby didn't answer. His eyes were still tight shut. The mower swirled round the last patch of grass, then stopped.

"Quick!" I said. "Quick! We've got to float him back!"

We all pointed our star fingers and thought of the lightest things we could – clouds and balloons and seagulls…

Nothing happened.

Well, something did, but it wasn't what we'd hoped for. Mr Appleby's eyes flicked open and he stared and he stared and he stared.

Sophie clutched my arm. "What on earth are we going to do now?"

Mr Appleby's face was scarlet, and his eyes were popping out of his head. He slowly got off his mower and scowled at it as if it was the mower's fault for being in

95

someone else's garden. Then he turned to the old lady, and he was almost spitting with rage. "How ... how ... how..." he began, but he couldn't even finish the sentence. He was so angry that he looked as if he was about to explode.

"Who is it?" The old lady was still standing by the back door of the house. "Who's there?"

"Oops," Sophie murmured.

My stomach was tied up in horribly painful knots. What had we done?

"NOW!" I thought. "It has to be NOW..." And I pointed my star finger. *"Memory hold not, memory care not..."* A shower of tiny glittery stars swirled around Mr Appleby's head.

As I said the words of the charm, my friends from Team Starlight joined in with

me. *"Memory slip slide slither away…"*

The change in Mr Appleby was extraordinary. One minute he was shaking with fury, and the next he didn't know what to do or what to say. He cleared his throat. "Ahem."

The old lady put out her hand to feel for her chair and took a couple of wobbly steps forward. "I heard the mower. Are you our neighbour?"

Mr Appleby opened his mouth, then closed it again. He took another look at his motor mower, then at the neatly mown lawn. He patted his chest as if to make sure that he was really there, and finally he gave his face a rub, as if he was trying to wake himself up. "Ahem," he said again. "Yes. Yes, I'm George Appleby. From next door. Excuse me … I find myself a little confused today. Did you ... that is, did you ask me to cut your grass?"

"Ask you? Goodness me, no!" The old lady gave Mr Appleby a huge smile. "I get a little confused myself sometimes. It's all part of getting old. You came round with the mower yourself."

Melody kicked my ankle, but I took no notice. I wanted to hear what the old lady was saying.

"You must have the kindest heart in all the world," she went on, "and we are the luckiest people to live next door to you."

Mr Appleby rubbed his face again, as if he still couldn't believe what was happening, but he was beginning to look happy. So happy, in fact, that I wondered how long it was since anybody had been pleased to see him ... and I felt an uncomfortable pang of

99

guilt. Whenever I met him, I ran away.

"Did I?" he said. "Did I come round with the mower? Well, I suppose I must have done. Goodness me! I'll be forgetting my own name next!" And, positively glowing, Mr Appleby walked over and shook the old lady's hand. "I'm pleased to meet you!"

"I've just made a pot of tea," she said. "Do say you'll come in and have a cup. My daughter will want to thank you. It's the most wonderful thing that you've done; the children will be able to play in the garden now." She put her hand on Mr Appleby's arm. "You must think we're dreadful neighbours. The baby crying all the time, and the boys playing football indoors. I'm sure they've been driving you mad. I'm so sorry."

We held our breath.

"No, no!" Mr Appleby sounded surprised. "Not at all!" The old lady was trying to lead him inside, but he stopped to glance at the overgrown flower beds. "I could help you with your weeding too. My garden's well under control, and I've plenty of spare time…"

Chapter Ten

As Mr Appleby closed the door behind him, we let out the loudest cheer ever. If he'd been in the garden, he'd have heard us for sure – and somebody did! Two little faces peeped out from an upstairs window, saw the garden and disappeared. A moment later, the two boys – I'm guessing they were about six and seven – came hurtling out of the house, clutching a football.

"Fantastic!" shouted one.

"Super duper!" yelled the other.

They were followed by their mother, Poppy. She was looking puzzled, but when she saw the tidied garden and the mown lawn she stood very still.

"Isn't it great, Mum?" asked the boys.

"Yes," she said. "Yes. It's ... it's a miracle." And she burst into tears, and rushed back into the house. A moment later, we could see her through the kitchen window, and she was HUGGING Mr Appleby! And he was looking THRILLED!

"That's the best result ever," Madison said. "I do so love happy endings!"

"Me too," said Lily, and Sophie nodded.

Ava was looking at Olivia. "What are you thinking?" she asked. "You're very quiet."

"I'm not sure," Olivia said. "I think maybe we're lucky that Mr Appleby is so nice."

"What do you mean?" Melody asked.

"Well..." Olivia rubbed her nose. "What if Mr Appleby had been horrible? We made him forget how he got into the garden, but we didn't make him into a kind man. Fairy Mary told us when we first got to the Academy. Spells can't do that. You can't change a bad person into a good one."

I was beginning to see what Olivia meant. A horrible Mr Appleby would have stomped away ... but he hadn't. In fact, he'd offered to go on helping with the garden. He was a nice man, and I'd never noticed. A nice man, but a man who talked a lot.

"Such a great deal of thinking, Miss Emma," said a voice, and I spun round. Professor Moth was leaning against the glass wall of the Travelling Tower, smiling at me. Fairy Fifibelle Lee was there too, and so was Fairy Mary.

"Oh!" I said, and I remembered the murmuring voices. "Have you been here all the time?"

Fairy Fifibelle nodded. The professor said, "Most interesting it has been."

Jackson nudged Melody, and Melody wrinkled her nose as if she wasn't thrilled.

I was surprised that Fairy Mary didn't talk to us about what we'd been doing on our mission like she usually does; all she did was click her fingers. "Time to go back to the Academy," she said.

At once the TT began to float upwards.

As we went, Fairy Fifibelle began waving her wand at the ground beneath.

"What are you doing?" I asked.

"Just a little tidying up, dearest heart," she said. "Look down!"

I looked, and I saw that Mr Appleby's gate was swinging open and there was a trail of grass between his house and the house next door. "OH!" I said. "You've made it look as if he drove his mower round!"

"We don't want him lying awake at night worrying," Fairy Mary said, and she sounded rather serious.

"Indeed, that would not be a happy ending," the professor agreed.

Melody frowned. "The garden's sorted and everyone's happy – what's the problem?"

"Yes," Jackson said, and she gave me a questioning look. "Aren't you going

107

to thank me and Melody? If we hadn't floated your Mr Appleby over the fence there wouldn't have been a happy ending, would there? You'd still be talking about what to do."

Fairy Mary held up her hand. "One moment, Jackson. If it hadn't been for Emma's quick thinking, and her excellent use of the Forgetting Spell, it could have been a catastrophe."

"But she wouldn't stop dithering," Melody argued. "If we hadn't done something, the garden would still be a mess."

Fairy Mary sighed. "But you didn't think through what you were doing, and a Stargirl has to be certain that her spell will always work for the best. Did you consider Mr Appleby's feelings? Did you check your plan with the other Stargirls?"

Melody shrugged. "No. But I still think we did a good job."

"Is this what Olivia was talking about?" Jackson was struggling to understand. "That we were lucky Mr Appleby was nice?"

"Yes," Fairy Mary said.

Jackson shook her head. "I don't get it. If it all ends up fine, isn't that OK?"

Fairy Mary sighed again. "I'm afraid not. Your actions today have not been as I would have wished. I will not expel you and Jackson from the Academy, but I do ask you to go home and think about what it means to be a Stargirl."

Melody looked at Jackson, and Jackson looked at Melody.

"But we will be allowed to come back, won't we?" Jackson asked.

"Yes," Fairy Mary opened the door of the

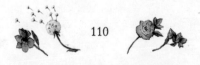

110

Travelling Tower, and we saw the familiar corridor that led away to the main rooms of the Academy. "We'll see you next time."

Melody walked to the doorway, then stopped, and I could see she was trying hard not to cry. "Please, Fairy Mary, will we get our fifth star?"

111

Fairy Mary shook her head, and a tear ran down Melody's cheek. She brushed it away as Jackson took her hand.

"Come on, Mel," she said. "It's not the end of the world. We're really good at magic. We'll win our stars next time." And the two of them walked away together.

As I watched Jackson and Melody go, I had a lump in my throat. Were they right? Would they manage to catch up?

Professor Moth knew what I was thinking. "It is hopeful that they will learn," he said, and he sounded sad too. "To be a Stargirl is very special – but the stars, they have to be earned."

"They do indeed," Fairy Mary said. "And some of you have done well today." I looked down at my pendant to see my stars ... and I gave a little squeak of

excitement. My fifth star was shining! It was shining so brightly I was almost dazzled. "That's amazing," I said. "Look at your pendants, everybody!"

All my friends' stars were shining too. "One more to go," Ava said. "Wow!"

113

"Will the last one be the hardest?" Sophie asked.

"It will be a Shimmering Spell," Fairy Fifibelle told her. "They can be tricky, but I'm sure my darling girls will manage."

"There can be no doubt about it," the professor said cheerfully. "And now we must return to see if the truly wonderful Miss Scritch has another small snack prepared." He rubbed his stomach. "I have the hollow in my belly!"

Chapter Eleven

I don't know quite how the professor managed it, but he ate almost as much of the spread Miss Scritch had waiting for us as he had earlier on in the day. Miss Scritch was SO pleased! She beamed every time he took another helping, and she went very pink indeed when he told her the meringues were the best he'd ever tasted – and he ate at least six. As Madison said, he was magic at eating as well as at spells.

I didn't feel very hungry, though. Fairy Fifibelle Lee saw me refuse a slice of my favourite cake, and she asked me if I was all right. "Yes," I said. "I'm really really REALLY pleased I've got my fifth star ... but I do sort

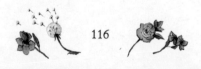

of wish Melody and Jackson were here too."

I knew as soon as I finished speaking that I'd get a hug, and I did. Once I'd recovered and untangled myself from Fairy Fifibelle's scarves and ribbons, she gave me a serious look. "Don't forget that Melody and Jackson have been given another chance, my precious petal," she said. "We do believe in them ... but perhaps it will take them a little longer to earn their stars."

That made me feel better. I ate my cake, and while I was eating it, I noticed that the professor had moved on from the meringues and was now chomping his way through a bag of apples.

"Apples!" I thought, and remembered that I'd brought them into the Academy when I first arrived that morning. It seemed ages ago, but I knew that as soon as I walked

out of the Academy, I'd be right back
where I'd been ... and that was exactly
what happened.

When it was time to go home, I walked
down the corridor and through the door –
and there I was in our messy back room.

119

There was one thing that was different, though. The bag that I was carrying was empty; there wasn't a single apple in it.

I heard Mum calling me, and I ran outside. She was still standing at the fence, but Mr Appleby was on the other side, beaming as if he'd won a million pounds.

"Emma!" Mum said. "Would you believe

it? Mr Appleby's tidied up the garden next door! He went round with his motor mower earlier on – nobody saw him go – and he's mowed the lawn! Isn't that incredibly kind of him?"

"Yes," I said, and I gave Mr Appleby my very best smile. "I think that's wonderful." I turned to Mum. "Is it OK if I pop round

and say hello to the new family sometime?"

"Of course." It was Mum's turn to smile. "By the way, what did you do with those apples? I've promised Mr Appleby a bagful."

"I'll pick some for him," I said. "I'll pick the nicest." And I did. And after I'd handed them over, and he'd thanked me, I went to see our new neighbours ... and the baby was a total darling. What's more, she stopped crying when I held her, and her mum said that I must be magic!

"Yes," I thought. "I am magic – just a tiny bit." And I touched my pendant under my T-shirt, and the baby looked at me and laughed.

Emma's Secret Code

Can you help us solve the secret code?

FORGETTING

SPELL

Answer:
FORGETTING
SPELL

Emma Piefold

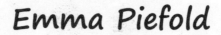

Loves:
Chatting!

Hates:
Being on
her own

**Favourite
colour:**
Yellow

Starsign:
Gemini

Secret fact:
She's named
after a
book

Stargirl Academy

One Token

www.stargirlacademy.com

Stargirl Academy

One Token

www.stargirlacademy.com

Stargirl Academy

One Token

www.stargirlacademy.com

Collect your FREE Stargirl Academy gifts!

In each Stargirl Academy book you will find three special star tokens that you can exchange for free gifts. Send your tokens in to us today and get your first special gift, or read more Stargirl Academy books, collect more tokens and save up for something different!

3 Tokens Bookmark

7 Tokens Star rubber

15 Tokens Set of star transfers

5 Tokens Sparkly pencil

13 Tokens Door hanger

Come back later, I'm reading

Stargirl Academy

WALKER BOOKS

Send your star tokens along with your name and address and the signature of a parent or guardian to:
Stargirl Academy Free Gift, Marketing Department,
Walker Books, 87 Vauxhall Walk, London, SE11 5HJ
Closing date: 31 December 2013

A message from Olivia

If you've read this book, you must like reading. I do too, and I'd be so pleased if you decide to read my story as well. It's about my poor cousin Hannah; she went to a new school, and things didn't go right for her at all. She REALLY needed help! My wonderful Stargirl friends were happy to come to the rescue, but then I messed everything up ... oh dear. See you soon, I hope —

Olivia xxx